Quentin Fenton Herter ~~III~~ THREE

by Amy MacDonald
Pictures by Giselle Potter

MELANIE KROUPA BOOKS
FARRAR, STRAUS AND GIROUX • NEW YORK

For my mother, who helped invent Quentin
many years ago
A.M.

For Keir
G.P.

Text copyright © 2002 by Amy MacDonald
Illustrations copyright © 2002 by Giselle Potter
Distributed in Canada by Douglas & McIntyre Ltd.
Color separations by Hong Kong Scanner Arts
Printed and bound in the United States of America by Worzalla
Designed by Jennifer Browne
First edition, 2002
1   3   5   7   9   10   8   6   4   2

Library of Congress Cataloging-in-Publication Data
MacDonald, Amy.
    Quentin Fenton Herter III / by Amy MacDonald ; illustrations by Giselle Potter.— 1st ed.
       p. cm.
    Summary: Quentin Fenton Herter Third is always perfectly behaved, but his shadow,
Quentin Fenton Herter Three, is quite the opposite.
       ISBN 0-374-36170-3
       [1. Behavior—Fiction. 2. Stories in rhyme. 3. Humorous stories.] I. Potter, Giselle, ill.
II. Title.

PZ8.3.M146 Qu 2002
[E]—dc21   2001027284

Quentin Fenton Herter Third
was seldom seen and never heard.

He always did what he should ought
and never did what he should not.

He never spoke till spoken to.
He closed his mouth in time to chew.

He always cleaned his supper plate
and went to bed each night at eight.

He kissed his aunts and cousin, too,
and bowed and asked, "How do you do?"

H e put his toys where they should go,
and never *ever* answered "No!"

Remembered always to say "Please,"
to wash behind his ears and knees.

H e never ran but always walked,
and sat quite still when grown-ups talked.

Oh, seldom seen and never heard
was Quentin Fenton Herter Third.

BUT...

Quentin Fenton had a Shadow:
never good and always bad! Oh,

he was bad as bad can be,

was Quentin Fenton Herter Three.

Yes, Quentin's Shadow answered back
and always took the last at snack.

H e interrupted left and right.
He never went to bed at night.

His friends he chivvied, teased, and bossed.
And—sad but true—he never flossed!

His toys he quite refused to share.
He never brushed his teeth or hair,

said "Please" or "Thanks" or "Ladies first."
And once—I'm told—he might have cursed.

(Oh, yes, he tried a naughty word—
unlike Quentin Fenton Third.)

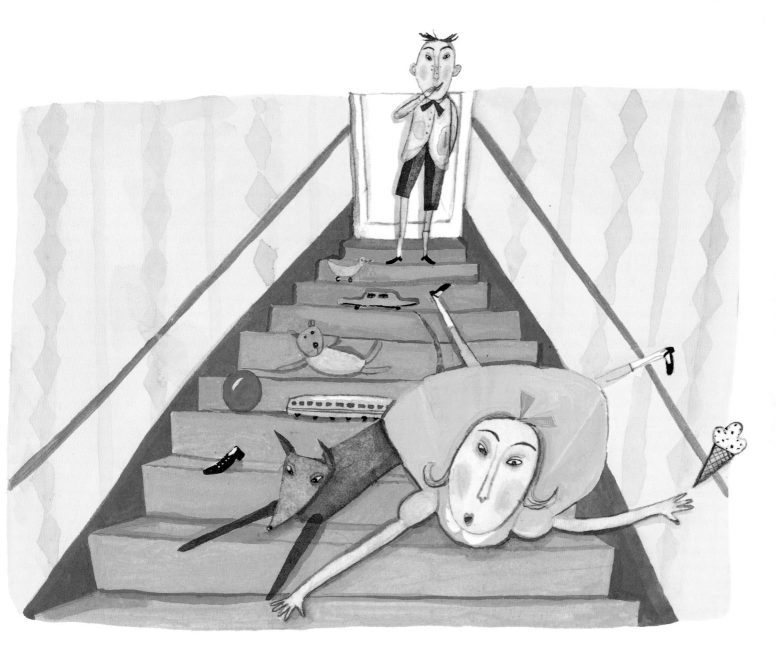

e sometimes lied, forgot his prayers,
left toys outside, or on the stairs.

He often tried to skip his chores,
and yawned out loud in front of bores.

He spilled his pudding on the floor
and wrote with crayon on the door.

In short, he did what he should not,
and never did what he should ought.

Oh, he was bad as bad can be,
was Quentin Fenton Herter Three.

Now...

Here's the funny thing about
the Quentins. You will laugh no doubt.

They loathed each other cordially,
did Quentin **Third** and Quentin Three.

BUT ...

What Quentin Third would not admit:
He wanted to be bad—a bit.

To throw a tiny little fit.
To drive his mother mad. (Admit:
You've often—you, too—thought of it.)

Whoever thought *he* could be naughty?
No, not Quentin! Not him! Not he!

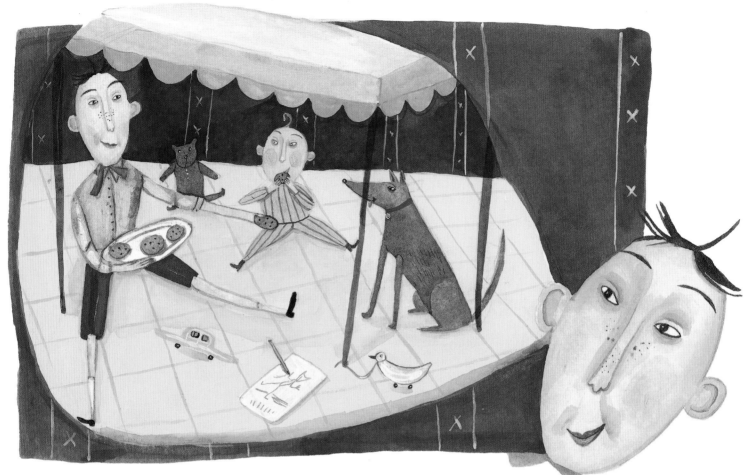

AND ...

What Quentin Three would not admit:
He longed to do some good—a bit.

A tiny tad, enough to show
he wasn't *always* bad, you know.

Whoever thought *he* could be good? He
really should—but would he? Could he?

THEN ...

Quentin went to tea one day
with Cousin Bea and Great-aunt May.

He crooked his pinky as he drank,
said "Yes, ma'am," "No, ma'am," "Please," and "Thank

you". . . Till, among the sticky buns,
the doilies, dust, and aged ones,

surrounded by Aunt Eloise,
the crumpets, scones, three kinds of teas,

he felt an urgent need to sneeze!

A first premonitory sniff
(where *was* his pocket handkerchief?).

His aunties eyed him, stern and rapt,
and . . . something inside Quentin snapped.

He stood up straight and opened wide.
(His aunts were frankly horrified.)

And Shadow (Quentin Herter Three)
cried, "Not right here! Not in the tea!"

But to him Quentin Third replied,
"[a naughty word I can't confide]."

H e breathed in deep ("Oh, my! Egad!")
and
S N E E Z E D

with all the sneeze he had!

The scene was like an atom blast.
The ladies stood (like you) aghast
amid remains of their repast.

O f Quentin Third, it's safe to say:
He was both seen *and* heard that day.

And (strange but true) when, in disgrace,
they sent him home, who took his place . . .

but Shadow! Strange, but true, you see,
for *he* behaved quite perfectly.

AND...

From that day, they made amends,
and Quentin Three and Third were friends.

Inseparable were Quent and Shad.

BUT...

were they GOOD? Or were they BAD?

The answer is, as you might guess,
a loud, resounding, heartfelt . . .

YES!

Yes, they were bad as good can be—
both Quentin **Third** and Quentin *Three*.